Picture Poems

Special thanks to: Shadow Projects, Shadow Character Design, and Shadow Digital

Designed by Charles Kreloff

Based on the Pooh stories by A. A. Milne (copyright The Pooh Properties Trust).

Printed in the United States of America

First Edition

Library of Congress Card Number: 2001090381

ISBN 0-7868-3341-6

For more Disney Press fun, visit www.disneybooks.com

Disney's

The Book of Pooh

Rebus Rhymes

Picture Poems

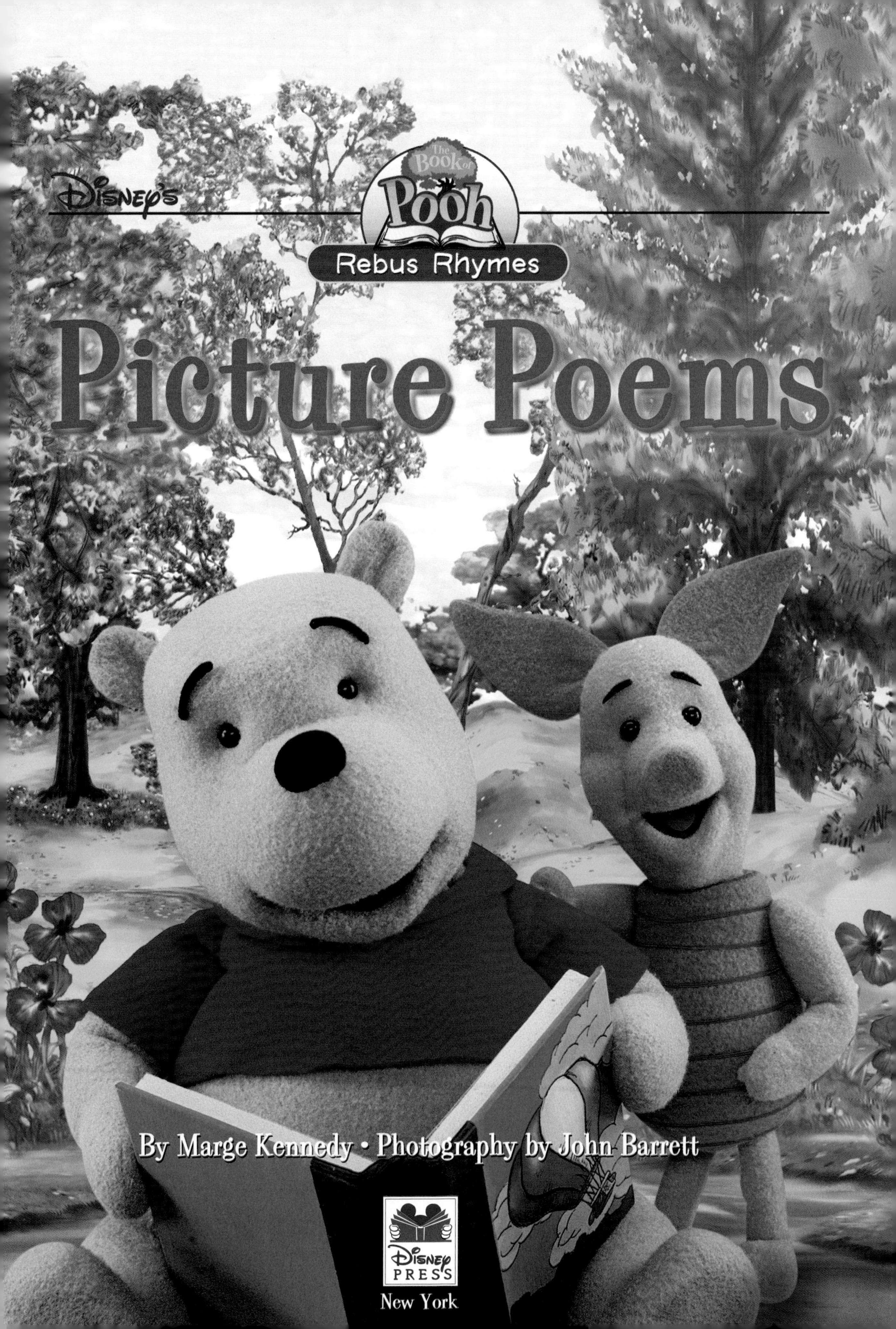

By Marge Kennedy • Photography by John Barrett

Disney Press
New York

Fun with **Picture Poems**!

Picture Poems makes learning to read fun with simple rebus rhymes about Pooh and his friends!

Here are some ways for your child to learn and have fun while reading **Picture Poems** with you!

"Read" the pictures.

First, look through **Picture Poems** with your child to find all of the pictures that replace nouns in the poems. Help your child name each picture he or she sees.

Read the poems.

As you read each poem, pause to give your child time to name the pictures in each one. The next time around, your child will pick up the rhythm and rhyme of the poems and the words will come faster.

Take turns reading!

After a few readings, take turns! Let your child read a poem to you. Then you read the next, and so on. "Reading" the pictures and completing the rhymes in each poem give your child the wonderful feeling of *"Hey! I can read!"*

5

Pooh Wakes Up

A  buzzed, "Good morning!"

 stretched and said,

"It's time to get up!"

So 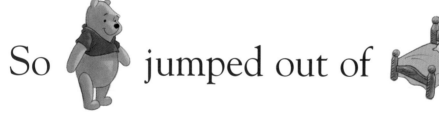 jumped out of  .

What will Pooh do when his feet hit the floor?
Just turn the page to see what's in store.

Pooh Gets Dressed

 chose his red shirt,

And a  for his head.

 looked in the .

"How handsome!" he said.

Pooh's tummy is rumbly for a sweet, tasty treat.
What will he find in the kitchen to eat?

Pooh Eats Breakfast

 went to the

Where he found a good treat:

Some  and some .

 sat down to eat.

Who will Pooh meet when he goes out to play?
Which friend is bouncing by Pooh's door today?

Tigger Visits Pooh

Outside,  shouted,

"Helloooo, my friend  !

I'm visiting  !

Would you like to come, too?"

Tigger keeps bouncing. Pooh tags along.
Will they find their friend Piglet before very long?

Piglet Draws a Picture

What's  drawing?

It looks like a  .

What will he draw next?

Will he draw a  ?

He's nearly finished. It's been so much fun!
Just turn the page to see what he's done.

Piglet Draws Some More

A  in the sky!

Some  that grow!

An 🍦, a 🌙 !

It's Piglet's art show!

The morning has ended. It's now time for lunch.
Who's bringing food from his garden to munch?

Rabbit Brings Lunch

 pushed his

Right through the  ,

He brought  and

For everyone's plate.

Who's rushing to meet him? Look up in the sky.
Is it Kessie or Owl who's flying so high?

Kessie Arrives!

Kessie flew from her

Singing, "Please wait for me!

I'd like some  ,

A 🍩 , and tea."

As soon as they all eat their last bite,
Owl decides that he will recite.

Owl Reads a Poem

" are red,

Except when they're blue,

If I weren't

Then I might be you."

His friends tiptoe off, as he reads from his chair:
"If I weren't here, then I might be there."

Pooh Hears a Sound

Later that day,

Heard a strange sound.

He stood by his

And he looked all around.

What does Pooh hear? Is the sound from his tummy?
Perhaps Pooh Bear needs a treat that is yummy.

Pooh Eats Dinner

"My tummy was rumbling,"  said to himself.

He reached for some

From his shelf.

After his dinner, what will Pooh do?

Take a bath, sing a song, or count up to two?

Pooh Goes to Bed

 put on his

And climbed into  ,

He blew out the

And lay down his head.

Pooh falls asleep and dreams, one by one,
Of each of his friends and the ways they've had fun.

Pooh's Picture Pages

The fun isn't over yet! How many of these picture words can you find in this book?

Pooh

bee

table

toast

tree

Tigger

mirror

gate

honey

flowers

sun

hat

Rabbit

wagon

Piglet

apples

bed

Owl

door

ice cream

nest

lettuce

yo-yo

roses

pajamas

carrots

candle

doughnut

31

More Fun with **Picture Poems!**

Rhyme together!

Look through the picture words on *Pooh's Picture Pages*. Can your child think of a real or nonsense word that rhymes with each one? (i.e., *hat: bat, fat, sat, lat; honey: money, funny, dunny*)

Name that sound!

Together, say the name of each picture in *Pooh's Picture Pages*. What beginning sound does each picture begin with? Which words begin with b, d, s, h, t, and so on?

What happens next?

Read the poems again—but this time with a twist! As you read the questions that follow each poem, does your child remember "what happens next" before you turn the page?